Ring Around a Mystery

Elizabeth Bryan Mysteries

Vicki Berger Erwin

For Carol Gorman, one of my favorite authors

Thanks to Dawn Weinstock
for her attention to detail
and to Ruth Geisler
for her continued support.

Elizabeth Bryan Mysteries

The Disappearing Card Trick
The Case of the Questionable Cousin
The Catnapping Caper
Ring Around a Mystery
Who Kidnapped Jesus?
The Secret in the Old Book

Cover illustration by Sally Schaedler

3558 S. Jefferson Avenue, St. Louis, MO 63118-3968
Manufactured in the United States of America

Library of Congress Cataloging-in-Publication Data
Ervin, Vicki Berger, 1951—
Ring around a mystery/Vicki Berger Erwin.
P. cm.—(Elizabeth Bryan mysteries;4)
Summary: After Justin is accused of stealing the friendship ring he gave her, Elizabeth attempts to help him by joining a clique of "party-up girls" who are also shoplifters.
ISBN 0-570-04886-9
[1. Shoplifting—Fiction. 2. Christian life—Fiction. 3. Mystery and detective stories.] I. Title. II. Series.
PZ7.E7445Ri 1997
[Fic]—dc20 96-9634

---

2 3 4 5 6 7 8 9 10 11 08 07 06 05 04 03 02 01 00 99

CONTENTS

1 WITNESS

"How many girls in our class are wearing those friendship rings?" Elizabeth asked Meghan.

"There are four in my homeroom and another one in my English class," Meghan answered.

The girls stared at a display of rings and earrings in the window of the newly opened Ring Doodle jewelry shop.

"What would your mom say if Justin gave you one?" Meghan asked, a mischievous smile on her face.

Elizabeth felt a blush creep up her cheeks. It still amazed her how her best friend managed to know exactly what she was thinking. And she *had* been thinking about what it would be like to wear a ring given to her by a boy—but not just any boy, Justin. She'd spent months insisting that Justin was a friend who happened to be a boy, but now she was wondering if that friend might give her a ring that meant something more. And did she really want that?

"I like them, but there's no chance some boy is going to spend that much money on a ring for me," Meghan said.

Elizabeth shrugged, glad that Meghan hadn't demanded an answer for her previous question.

"Do you want to go inside?" asked Meghan.

"Sort of," Elizabeth said, "but look who's already here."

"Party-up girls," Meghan whispered, using the code phrase she and Elizabeth had given the three girls crowded around the display counter. Christy, Heather, and Sarah talked constantly about giving and going to parties. They called each other "my fellow PUGs" and marked all their belongings with the initials. What *PUG* stood for, no one knew for sure.

All five girls went to North Middle School and belonged to the same church. Even before they started nursery school together, Meghan and Elizabeth had celebrated birthdays with Christy and slept over at one another's houses.

Then they reached middle school and boys became a bigger part of the picture.

"I wonder what really goes on at their parties," Meghan said.

"Maybe we'll be invited to the next one. Christy's mom still asks my mom why I never come over anymore."

"It's weird. I still miss Christy sometimes, you know? We had a lot of fun," said Meghan.

"In the good old days," Elizabeth added. They both laughed.

Meghan pushed the door of the jewelry store open and motioned for Elizabeth to follow. Elizabeth ran her hand through her long, red hair, wishing she'd taken time to brush it.

Christy's eyes met Elizabeth's as she walked inside. Elizabeth smiled, and Christy quickly turned to Sarah and whispered.

"These are the rings all the guys are giving to the girls they like," Meghan said, dragging Elizabeth with her to a glass case near the three PUGs.

Elizabeth tried to shake off Christy's cold reception. Christy was the only one of the three girls who still came to the church youth group. At the activities, Christy was always friendly to

Elizabeth and Meghan, but when the other PUGs were around, it was a different story. Elizabeth told herself to get over it and leaned her head close to Meghan's.

The friendship rings were wide gold and silver bands with words or phrases engraved on them in fancy script. *Love* said one; *Forever* said another. A few had colored stones embedded above each letter.

"I get it," said Elizabeth after studying the stone-studded bands. "The *D* has a diamond above it, the *E* an emerald, *A* has amethyst, *R* gets a ruby. The stones spell out the word too."

"Cool," said Meghan. "I like those even better than the engraved ones."

A salesclerk had lined up tray after tray of rings in front of Christy and her friends. The woman turned toward Elizabeth and Meghan. "I'll be there in a minute," she said.

"Just looking," Elizabeth called back.

The door opened, signalled by a flat tinkling of the tune "Ring-around-the-Rosey." A man wearing a navy blue suit, a baseball hat, and mirrored sunglasses stepped up to the counter next to Elizabeth and looked at the rings.

Elizabeth wondered how he could see much wearing sunglasses inside the store. He slowly circled the counter, apparently fascinated by the rings and earrings. The man stood out in the crowd of young girls and women.

The bell played its tune again, causing a flurry of excitement among the PUGs. Christy's hand went to her shiny, brown hair, flipping it over her shoulder. Sarah glanced at Christy and elbowed Heather. The two of them giggled as Christy smiled brightly at the newcomer. Elizabeth turned to see who it was.

Justin and his friend Matt stood in the doorway, their eyes darting from one display to another. When Justin's eyes landed on Elizabeth, he visibly relaxed.

"You can help me," he said, joining her. Matt leaned against the end of the counter, glancing at Christy, Heather, and Sarah, then at the floor.

"What are you doing here?" Meghan asked slyly, looking at Elizabeth, then at the tray of rings.

Justin took off his baseball cap, pushed his blond hair off his forehead, then stuck the cap on top of it. "It's my mom's birthday, and I need to get her something. Earrings, I guess." As he continued to look around the room, Justin's shoulders slumped lower and lower. "I didn't know there were so many kinds."

"Do you remember what happened when you went shopping with me for my mom's birthday?" Elizabeth asked.

"We ended up in *another* mystery," said Justin, referring to the catnapping Elizabeth, Meghan, and he had helped solve. Justin looked around again, rubbed the back of his neck nervously, then stuck his hand in his pocket. "I thought they had earrings in here, but all I see are rings."

Elizabeth looked down the counter again. Matt still hadn't come close enough to get in on the conversation. He didn't even seem to know Elizabeth and Meghan were in the store. Christy was smiling at Justin as she twisted a piece of hair around her finger. Elizabeth moved a step closer to Justin.

"What do you think? one of these?" Justin pointed at the rings Elizabeth and Meghan had been admiring.

"These aren't for mothers," said Meghan. Justin's brow wrinkled.

"Are your mom's ears pierced?" Elizabeth asked quickly. She didn't want Meghan to say anything else about the rings.

"Yeah, I think so."

Elizabeth pointed to a display of gold earrings—hoops, dangles, and geometric shapes—on another counter. The man with the sunglasses was partly blocking their way, so Elizabeth, followed by Justin, squeezed between the man and a table so they could get to the earrings.

The man's hand rested on top of several cards of earrings that had fallen off a display rack on to the counter. Elizabeth hoped he wasn't covering up something Justin might like.

At first she thought nothing of the flash that she saw out the corner of her eye. Elizabeth pointed at several pairs of earrings she thought Justin's mom would like. Then she heard something drop to the floor. Elizabeth looked to make sure she hadn't knocked a card off the counter. The man with the sunglasses had squatted down. Elizabeth saw a second flash arc into the man's pocket, then she realized he was stuffing cards of gold earrings into his coat.

The man's head whipped up. Elizabeth could feel his eyes behind the dark glasses lock onto her face. It was almost like he was daring her to say something as he memorized her features. She couldn't move, so chilling was his sightless gaze.

Springing up, the man turned quickly and made his way to the door. Elizabeth opened her mouth to call out to someone to stop the man. Before the words could come out, he turned and stared at her again. Her mouth snapped shut. At that moment, Elizabeth knew what it meant to be frozen with fear.

The man had almost reached the door by the time Elizabeth figured out what to do. She looked around for someone who worked in the store. The only clerk in sight was deep in conversation with a customer at the necklace counter.

Leaving Justin staring after her, Elizabeth rushed to the counter. "Excuse me," she said, interrupting the woman's explanation of gold content. The salesclerk turned cold eyes on Elizabeth.

"A man. Wearing sunglasses. He took some earrings." Elizabeth pointed toward the exit. The man had the door open a crack.

"You!" the woman called without hesitation. "Stop!"

2

THE ACCUSED

Silence dropped on the store like a curtain. The man glanced over his shoulder, and Elizabeth again felt the jarring power of his hidden gaze as he jerked the door open. "Ring-around-the-Rosey" accompanied his getaway.

Several customers rushed to the door and watched as he jogged away. Elizabeth took a step toward the door. "Aren't you going to go after him? or call the police?" she asked the clerk.

"Why didn't you come get me sooner?" the woman asked, turning on Elizabeth, anger coloring her words.

Again Elizabeth couldn't make a sound come out of her mouth. She'd thought she'd done something good by alerting the clerk. Sure she had hesitated a moment, worried that the man might know that she was the one who'd turned him in, but she had come forward.

"He's gone now. Another shoplifter gets away with it." The woman turned her back on Elizabeth and said something in low tones to the customer she'd been helping. The customer, an older woman, looked at Elizabeth and shook her head.

Elizabeth's face burned. She felt like she was the guilty one. People throughout the store were whispering to one another.

"Hey, you tried," Justin said as he came up behind Elizabeth. "I didn't even see what was happening."

"I wish I hadn't," said Elizabeth. "He knew that I saw him, and when he looked at me ..." she shivered.

"It's okay," said Justin. He patted her on the shoulder.

"What do you think of these earrings?" He held up a pair with dangling golden rings. "Kind of expensive, aren't they?"

"They're gold," Elizabeth explained. "Some of the others may be a littler cheaper."

Moving to a second counter, Justin and Elizabeth looked through more earrings. Elizabeth checked to see where Meghan had gone. She was still at the ring counter. And Christy was still eyeing Justin even though Matt was trying to talk to her. It made Elizabeth want to grab Justin's arm, but she knew he would think she'd gone nuts.

"I still like that first pair best," said Justin. He removed one of the dangling earrings and held it up to Elizabeth's ear. "What do you think?"

"Cute," said Elizabeth. She'd gotten a look at the price—$38.

"Can I help you?" A second salesclerk had finally appeared and stepped to their side of the counter.

"These. I'll take these," Justin said.

"They're adorable, dear," the woman said to Elizabeth.

Elizabeth shook her head. "They're a birthday present. For his mom."

"What a darling boy you are," the clerk said. "I'll wrap them up real pretty for you."

Justin pulled his wallet out of his jeans pocket and opened it.

"Forty dollars and 48 cents," the woman said.

"Do you have 50 cents?" Justin whispered

to Elizabeth. She dug into her purse and found two quarters.

"Can we look at those rings while you're wrapping the present?" Meghan asked the salesclerk.

"I shouldn't ... the rule is ... I guess so," she finally said, pulling the stone-studded bands out of the case.

Meghan began trying on the rings one by one. "Which one do you like best?" she asked Elizabeth.

"This one, I guess." Elizabeth picked up the silver ring with *Dear* spelled out in script and stone.

Meghan slipped it on Elizabeth's finger. "A perfect fit. What do you think, Justin?"

He looked at the ring and shrugged. "Are those as expensive as earrings?"

Pulling the ring off, Elizabeth read the price written on the small tag and nodded. She replaced it in the tray.

"Lots of kids at school have rings like those," Justin said.

"Boys give them to the girls they are going out with," Meghan said, looking at Elizabeth.

"Oh." From the expression on Justin's face,

it was clear this was the first time he'd heard of the custom. He looked at the ring again and glanced sideways at Elizabeth. Elizabeth avoided looking at either Justin or the tray of rings.

The salesclerk returned, setting a silver-wrapped gift on the counter in front of Justin. "Finished?" she asked, as she started to put the rings away.

"Not quite," Meghan said. The woman put the tray back in front of Meghan and turned to Christy and her friends. The threesome had tried on dozens of rings and left them scattered over the counter before moving on to the earrings.

"I'd better go," said Justin, handling his mother's gift-wrapped package like it was burning his fingers. "Hey, Matt, ready?"

"See you tomorrow," said Elizabeth.

Justin left without, Elizabeth noted, looking back at Christy. Matt, however, stopped and waved through the window, setting off a storm of giggling from across the counter.

"Try that one again," Meghan said, tapping the *Dear* ring.

Before Elizabeth could remove the ring from the tray, Christy joined them. "Are you going out with Justin?" she asked.

"We're just friends," said Elizabeth, wanting to make it sound like more but knowing anything she said to Christy about Justin would be all over school by lunchtime tomorrow.

"But you were looking at these rings," Christy said.

"He was buying his mom a birthday present," explained Elizabeth.

"If you *were* getting a ring from the J-Man, which one would you want?" Christy asked.

The J-Man? Elizabeth thought.

"That one," Meghan answered for her friend, pointing to the *Dear* ring.

Christy nodded. She flipped her hair over her shoulder again and curled her lips up in a flat smile. "Good choice."

"We've got to go," Elizabeth said, wondering why Christy always managed to make her feel like her hair was greasy and her feet were too big—and everybody knew it.

"See you in church," Christy said much too sweetly.

Elizabeth grabbed Meghan's arm and pulled her away from the counter. Opening the door, she was grateful for the rush of cool air against her burning cheeks.

"You should have told her Justin was taken," said Meghan.

"How could I when it's not true?" Elizabeth asked.

"Stop it. He spends as much time with you as he does any of his guy friends," Meghan said.

"*Friend* is the key word there," Elizabeth said. "I've got to get home. You want to come too? I'm hungry for popcorn."

"I could go for some of that. You know, popcorn is a healthy, low-calorie snack as long as it doesn't have a lot of butter or oil."

"Since when do you care if something is healthy or low-calorie?" asked Elizabeth.

"I need to start watching what I eat. I think I'm going to be short forever, so the only place I can put extra calories is out." Meghan puffed out her cheeks.

"You don't have a thing to worry about," Elizabeth assured her.

"Isn't that Mr. Hamilton's car?" Meghan asked, pointing at a black Volvo parked alongside the curb.

Elizabeth nodded. Don Hamilton's car had become very familiar since he'd started going out with her mom and spending what seemed like most of his time at their house.

At first, Elizabeth hadn't liked him at all. Or, as she'd finally decided, she didn't like the idea of any man trying to take her dad's place. Over time Elizabeth hadn't been able to keep from liking him. He was nice, fun, even cute. Mom and Mike, Elizabeth's little brother, were crazy about the man. Elizabeth still wasn't sure she was ready to welcome him into the family, but she was willing to have him hang around as much as he wanted.

"I wonder where he is? Maybe we can get a ride home," said Elizabeth.

"Elizabeth, look!" Meghan stopped in the middle of the sidewalk. She squeezed Elizabeth's arm. "Your mom and Mr. Hamilton are in the jewelry story, and look what they're doing!"

Elizabeth looked at her mom's reddish-blonde head leaning close to Don Hamilton's dark curls as the two of them admired the diamond ring sparkling on the third finger of Mom's outstretched hand.

"Engagement rings!" Meghan breathed, twisting her long, dark braid between her fingers. "How romantic!"

Elizabeth tried to turn away, but she just

couldn't take her eyes off her mom and Don.

"Why didn't you tell me they were getting engaged?" Meghan poked her.

Elizabeth tried to swallow the lump in her throat. Hot tears burned her eyelids. Why hadn't anyone told *her?*

"Maybe we shouldn't wait around for a ride," said Meghan. "In fact, maybe I shouldn't go home with you after all. They won't want me there when they come in with the good news."

Mom and Don laughed as Mom tried on another ring.

"Maybe not," Elizabeth said.

"Call me and let me know what happens." Meghan smiled broadly and squeezed Elizabeth's arm again. She turned and ran back the way they'd come, giving Elizabeth a thumbs up before she disappeared around the corner.

Home. Elizabeth couldn't face the thought. She walked slowly, her backpack clutched tightly to her chest. At the corner she turned and circled the block. Don's car was still in front of the jewelry store, and Elizabeth realized she was in front of Ring Doodle. Staring at the window display, she was struck by the thought that *she* should be getting rings from boys, not her mother.

The store had emptied. Only the salesclerk who had yelled at her remained, busily straightening the counter. Elizabeth decided to try to set things straight with her. She opened the door, prompting the flat, tinkling tune.

Irritating, Elizabeth thought.

The salesclerk looked up, and the smile on her face dissolved when she saw Elizabeth. Her face darkened and her brow creased. "You!" she spat. "The nerve."

Elizabeth took a step backward and reached behind her for the door handle. What was going on?

"I want you and your friends to know that we will not tolerate shoplifters in this store. We *will* prosecute," the woman said.

"Shoplifter?" Elizabeth knew her lips had formed the word, but no sound came out.

"You and your friends were the last ones to look at that ring," the woman continued.

"Excuse me?" Elizabeth finally managed to say. Was the woman accusing *her* of shoplifting? "I don't know what you're talking about."

"The *Dear* ring. It's gone."

"And you think *I* took it?" Elizabeth's voice squeaked.

"You were trying it on the last time I saw it," the clerk said. "You thought you were pretty clever, accusing someone else of exactly what you were planning. And now, coming back in here all innocent."

Shaking her head, Elizabeth moved to the counter. The ring was gone. "Maybe it's on the floor or in another tray." She dropped to the floor, looking all around, even patting her hand along the carpet.

"It's gone," the woman said with certainty in her words.

"I didn't take it," Elizabeth said, rising. She'd never been accused of anything like this before and couldn't believe it was happening to her now. Help me know what to say, Jesus, she prayed silently.

The salesclerk's confidence in her accusation seemed to slip a notch in the face of Elizabeth's repeated denials.

"And my friends would never think of stealing either," Elizabeth said. "I admit I wish I'd been able to stop that man from taking the earrings, but if you'd seen the way he looked at me ... Really, I'd never steal anything."

The frown marking the woman's brow

relaxed a little more. "We've lost so much to shoplifters lately. I know our merchandise is small and it's a temptation ..."

"Not for me," Elizabeth interrupted the woman.

The salesclerk sighed. "These rings are all one of a kind. If you wear it, we'll know where you got it, and believe me, we'll be watching you all. You might pass the word along."

Did the woman believe her? Elizabeth wondered. She had seemed to back off a little from her accusation. Elizabeth didn't know what else she could say. She left the store wondering if she'd ever feel like she could return.

3

Secrets

When Elizabeth arrived home, there was no sign of Don Hamilton's car, and only a single light burned in the hallway. She wondered where Mom had stuck her brother while she was shopping for her engagement ring.

Elizabeth was surprised to find the door unlocked. She dumped her backpack on the seat of the hat tree, then hung her purse on one of the hooks surrounding the mirror.

"Did you have a good day?" Mom's voice coming out of the darkness sent a shiver of fear through Elizabeth until she realized who was speaking.

Mom turned on the reading lamp beside the recliner.

"It was okay," said Elizabeth, blinking until her eyes adjusted to the brightness.

"Where've you been?"

Elizabeth bristled, interpreting the question as an accusation. "I *told* you Meghan and I were going to check out that new jewelry store on the way home from school."

"That's right. You did." Mom smiled at her. "How was it?"

Like a weight descending on her, Elizabeth remembered the shoplifter she'd let get away and the salesclerk's accusation. What would Mom think of her being accused of stealing?

"Elizabeth, what's wrong?" Mom asked.

"Nothing," Elizabeth said. Why wasn't Mom showing her an engagement ring. "Why are you sitting here in the dark? Have you been sitting here ever since you got home from school? Is supper started?" Elizabeth knew the answers, but she wanted to hear what Mom would say.

"I'm resting, and, yes, I have been sitting here since I got home. What about the store?" Mom repeated.

"They have lots of cute stuff," Elizabeth said quickly.

"You don't sound too sure about that."

Elizabeth wanted to tell Mom what happened, to be reassured she'd done the right thing about the shoplifter and, most of all, that the salesclerk believed that she didn't take the ring. But Mom had her secrets, and maybe she didn't care about Elizabeth's.

"Where's Mike?" Elizabeth asked.

"With Aunt Nan."

"How come?"

As if he'd heard his name, Mike burst through the front door followed by Aunt Nan. "Look what we made," he shouted.

Elizabeth rubbed her ears as she looked at the bright-colored globs of clay on the tray Mike held up in front of her face.

"There's one for you, Lizbeth, and one for Mom, and one for me, and one for Aunt Nan, and one for ..."

"We get the picture," Elizabeth said, cutting Mike off.

Mom frowned at Elizabeth. "They're beautiful," she said to Mike, leaving unasked the question Elizabeth had on the tip of her tongue—what are they?

"Rings, Mom. They're rings. One for you, and one for Lizbeth, one for Aunt Nan ..."

Mom reached out and chose a red glob with yellow and blue dots on it. She slipped it on her finger and admired it.

Rings, thought Elizabeth. What was it with rings today? Watching Mom, Elizabeth experienced a wash of dread just like she'd felt earlier in the afternoon when she'd seen Mom in the jewelry store with Don—Mr. Hamilton.

As Mike pushed a pink ring on her finger, Elizabeth asked as casually as she could, "Where's Mr. Hamilton?"

"Mr. Hamilton?" Mom gave a short laugh. "You haven't called Don that for months."

"Well, where is he?" Elizabeth repeated in a demanding voice. It sounded rude even to her ears.

"He has a meeting at the high school," Mom answered.

"What did *you* do today?" Elizabeth continued in the same tone.

"Taught, ran a few errands," Mom said, still not mentioning the trip to the jewelry store. Elizabeth sighed loudly.

"What is the matter with you?" Aunt Nan asked, a sharp edge to her voice.

"Didn't have a good day," Elizabeth mumbled. She wanted to talk to somebody about what had happened at Ring Doodle. But Mom was keeping secrets, big secrets, so maybe she didn't feel like talking. Aunt Nan, who was their neighbor and like a grandmother to Elizabeth and Mike, didn't seem very sympathetic either.

"Do you like your ring?" Mike asked as he tugged on Elizabeth's hand.

Elizabeth looked down at the heavy clump of pink clay on her finger. Mike was looking at her with a yearning expression on his face, willing her to say something nice. She put her arm around him and gave him a quick hug. "It's beautiful," Elizabeth said. Besides, she thought, it's probably the only ring I'll ever get from a boy.

4 The J-Man's Surprise

"She didn't!" Meghan said to Elizabeth. They were walking past Ring Doodle on their way to Elizabeth's after-school job at the Read It Again bookstore. Meghan stopped beside the jewelry store's door.

"I don't want to go in," Elizabeth said in a whisper.

"Christy. It could have been her. She was still there when we left," said Meghan, also whispering.

"There were probably lots of people after us. And the ring was there when we left too. You know, the clerk said they were all one of a kind ..."

The door flew open and Matt barrelled out onto the sidewalk. "Whoa!" he said, stopping just short of knocking Elizabeth and Meghan down.

"Hi, Matt," the girls said in unison.

"You *didn't* see me here," Matt said. One hand was clenched shut, and his face was red. He stuffed his clenched hand into his pocket.

"No problem," said Meghan.

"I know how girls talk to each other, and I don't want to hear about this at school tomorrow," he growled.

Elizabeth had always thought Matt was a bully, and now she was sure of it. "We said we wouldn't," Elizabeth repeated. But she couldn't help wondering why he didn't want anyone to know he'd been at the store. Had Matt bought someone a ring? If he had, standing in front of the store window wasn't a good way to hide the fact.

"Weird guy," said Meghan as Matt walked off.

"Come on, I've got to get to work," said Elizabeth, pulling Meghan away from the jewelry store.

The girls parted at the door of the bookstore. "Don't keep worrying about what that woman said," Meghan said. "You know you didn't do it, and most important, God knows you didn't steal anything."

Elizabeth nodded. Meghan had a point. She was blessed to have such a good friend. And she had an idea. If the rings were unique, *she* could find who had taken it—if someone dared to wear it.

Stepping inside the bookstore, a large, fluffy gray cat wrapped herself around Elizabeth's legs in greeting. "Hi, Finola." Elizabeth leaned down and petted the cat. Then she called out, "Teresa, I'm here. Do you have any deliveries for me today?"

Elizabeth had started delivering books to Read It Again's customers when Teresa's brother had walked out on his job. It was a dream job for a book lover like Elizabeth—a little bit of spending money and all the books she could read. She also liked the owner, Teresa, and her cats. The cats had been a big part of the last mystery she'd solved.

A face encircled by orange-red curls appeared above a wobbling stack of books. "Hello, luv. No deliveries." Teresa set the books on a table and wiped her hands on the skirt of her denim jumper. "Would you like to help me find resting places for these books?"

An orange-striped cat jumped on the table

of books next to where Elizabeth stood, demanding attention. She stroked Duncan, then stashed her backpack behind the counter and joined Teresa.

"You look a little low," Teresa said.

"Do you have a problem with shoplifters?" Elizabeth asked.

"I doubt there is a retail establishment unplagued by thievery," Teresa answered.

Elizabeth took a book off the stack, looked at the author's name, then placed it on the shelf in proper order. The books were all romance titles, not one of her favorite categories. The shelving would go quickly since she wouldn't be tempted to read a little bit in each one. When she helped with mystery books, Elizabeth couldn't resist sampling. "Have you ever seen someone take something?" she asked.

"I've *suspected* people," Teresa answered.

"Did you accuse them?"

"Never! I would have to be absolutely certain, observe with my own eyes, to confront the culprit," Teresa stated.

Elizabeth sighed. Had the Ring Doodle salesclerk been so certain? "I saw someone take something at a store the other day, and he knew

I saw him. For a minute I was scared of what he'd do if I said anything. I couldn't. Say anything, I mean."

"That's understandable," Teresa said.

"But I did, finally, after the man was almost out of the store." Elizabeth sighed again. "And the salesclerk got so mad at me because he was gone ..." She grabbed another book and the entire stack toppled. Elizabeth threw up her hands.

"It's only books. Nothing damaged. We'll have it cleared in an instant," Teresa said, patting Elizabeth on the arm.

The door opened, and Elizabeth turned to see who was there.

"Thought you'd be here," Justin said.

"Hi," said Elizabeth.

"Welcome," Teresa said. "You chose an opportune time to arrive. Our girl needs cheering up. Perhaps the two of you could share a cup of tea."

Elizabeth had to grin at the thought of sipping a cup of tea with Justin. "I need to finish here," she said.

"I insist you go with your friend." Teresa put her hands on Elizabeth's shoulders and gave her a gentle shove.

"Are you sure?" Elizabeth asked.

"Go, go."

"I'll stop by tomorrow to see if you need help," Elizabeth promised as she retrieved her backpack from behind the counter.

"Fine," said Teresa. "See you then."

Justin held the door open for Elizabeth. "Want to go to the donut shop?" she asked. A chocolate donut and a few of Justin's bad jokes might make her feel better.

"Sure, in a minute." Justin stopped at the corner and looked all around. He took his baseball cap off, squeezed the bill, then stuck it back on his head.

"No cars. Let's go," said Elizabeth, stepping off the curb.

"No, no. Wait a minute. If I don't say this, ask you this, right now, I'm going to chicken out." Justin stuck his hand in his pocket. "Here."

Elizabeth still had one foot on the sidewalk and one in the street as she turned around to see why Justin was acting so weird.

The ring rested in the palm of his hand—the ring Elizabeth had been accused of stealing.

5

To Catch a Thief

"Where did you get that?" Elizabeth practically shouted.

"It's … I want … It's for you," Justin stammered.

Elizabeth could only stare at him. Ring Doodle claimed their rings were one of a kind, and she was sure this was the one she'd seen there the day before. It was engraved with the letters D-E-A-R. A colored stone was embedded above each letter—a diamond, an emerald, an amethyst, and a ruby.

"Boys give these rings to girls when they …" Justin's voice trailed off.

"But where did you get it?" Elizabeth finally managed to say. "At Ring Doodle?"

Justin closed his hand around the ring and pulled it away from her. "No. Those were … I couldn't afford those."

"Where?" she asked again.

"What does it matter?" Justin asked.

Justin couldn't. He wouldn't, Elizabeth thought. But the ring had been stolen from Ring Doodle and now Justin was trying to give it to her. He'd been in the shop at the same time she was there. He'd seen the ring.

Even while she battled the thought of Justin as a thief, the thought that Justin wanted to go out with *her* was making Elizabeth's pulse race.

"I can't," Elizabeth said. No matter how much she wanted the ring and what it meant, she couldn't take it knowing that .... It was hard to think about Justin and shoplifting together.

Justin's face turned red. He quickly put the ring back in his pocket. "I thought," he started, "never mind."

"Just tell me where you got the ring," Elizabeth tried one more time.

"Why?"

She took a deep breath. Elizabeth wasn't going to let being afraid stop her this time. She wasn't going to let another shoplifter get away with it.

"What? Why are you looking at me like

that?" Justin asked.

Elizabeth rubbed her head. Justin … shoplifter. It didn't fit. The hand in the pocket … *Matt's* hand stuffed in his pocket. Elizabeth gasped as the picture of the man who had stuffed the earrings in his pocket was replaced by a picture of Matt sticking his hand in his pocket.

"Elizabeth …"

"I went back to Ring Doodle yesterday afternoon, after the shoplifter, and the woman told me that this ring had been stolen."

Justin shook his head. "But the ring was there after that man ran out. Besides, I told you I didn't get it there."

"She accused me of taking it," Elizabeth said.

"You? That's ridiculous." Justin started to laugh, then stopped. "Wait a minute. You don't think …"

Elizabeth shook her head.

"But you did. For a minute, you thought …"

"The rings are one of a kind, and I knew this one was stolen," Elizabeth tried to explain. "I didn't really think …"

"You won't believe this, but I found it on the

floor at school. I should have turned it in at the office, but I didn't. Man, I saw how much you wanted it, and I'd been thinking about how I could make some extra money to get it for you. Then it was right there by my locker. I knew I shouldn't have." Justin glanced at Elizabeth, then quickly lowered his eyes to his shoes.

"Whoever stole it must have dropped it," Elizabeth said. "And they probably want it back." Elizabeth felt the excitement build as she realized that her plan to find the thief might actually succeed.

"If it's stolen, they wouldn't go to the school office to look for it," said Justin. "I didn't take it from the store. You believe me, don't you?"

"In my heart I knew you couldn't have taken it. But my eyes were looking at this ring I knew someone stole. Forgive me?" Elizabeth asked.

Justin grinned. "Hey, you keep telling me that Jesus forgives me for a lot worse things, so I can forgive you. Can *you* forgive that woman who accused you?"

Elizabeth knew, and she knew that Justin knew, he had her there. Her Sunday school teacher had just reminded her class that week that Jesus set an example for us by forgiving His enemies. "I'm going to find out who really took the ring so she'll know I didn't do it," Elizabeth said.

"But ..."

"Okay, okay. Yes, I think I'll be able to forgive her." Elizabeth also knew she'd need a little help from God to do it.

"Why don't we just take the ring back to the store?" Justin asked. "After all, it's probably just as bad to keep a ring you know is stolen as to steal the ring in the first place."

"We will take the ring back, once we know who took it. If I take it back now, the salesclerk will think I'm bringing it back because she knows I took it," said Elizabeth.

"How do you think you're going to be able to find out who took the ring?" Justin asked. "It could have been *anyone.*"

"It has to be someone we know," said Elizabeth. "Don't you think it's strange *you* found the ring?"

"For a very short time I thought it was lucky."

"Aunt Nan says there's no such thing as luck," Elizabeth said with a smile. "God makes good things happen. But even if the ring didn't find its way to you on purpose, the thief has to be someone we know from school. And we're going to find out who that person is."

6

An Invitation

The ring made Elizabeth's hand feel heavy. She felt self-conscious, like everyone in her English class was looking at it and knew where it had come from. But she kept telling herself she *had* to wear it. It was part of the plan.

"Elizabeth!" Christy squealed, then grabbed Elizabeth's hand. "Look at this, Heather, look."

Elizabeth tried to pull her hand away.

"It's Justin, isn't it? You're going out with Justin!" Christy was talking so loudly the entire class had turned to look. Most of the boys lost interest as soon as they figured out it was a girl thing, but the girls in the class gathered around, o-oohing and a-aahing over the ring.

Christy held her hand up and wiggled her fingers. "Me too!" A similar ring adorned her hand.

Heather looked at Elizabeth. "This calls for

a party—a celebration. My house. Friday night. Couples only. You and Justin are invited."

The invitation, bestowed so regally, took Elizabeth by surprise. "I'll see," Elizabeth said, a tiny seed of excitement planted itself in her—her first PUG party. She turned to Christy. "Who gave you yours?"

"Matt," Christy replied matter of factly.

Elizabeth's theory about who had stolen the *Dear* ring collapsed. If Matt had taken the ring, Christy would be wearing it instead of her. For a fleeting moment, Elizabeth thought about the impossibility of Justin finding this particular ring. Just as quickly she pushed the doubts aside.

"Class, please take your seats." Mrs. Eidson clapped her hands to get their attention.

"We'll talk later," Christy whispered as she took her seat.

For a moment Elizabeth let herself bask in the warm feeling of being the center of attention. She let herself enjoy what it would be like to really wear a ring Justin gave her. She thought about what it meant that Justin had offered her a friendship ring. She'd spent so much time wondering who had shoplifted the ring that she'd forgotten what it meant.

Elizabeth looked around the classroom. Was one of the kids sitting with her a thief?

"We got invited to a party, but I'm not any closer to figuring out who took the ring," Elizabeth reported to Justin when they met after school.

"A party? Where?"

"Heather's," said Elizabeth.

"Wow! A PUG party. I hear they get pretty wild. Wanna go?" Justin asked.

"Hey, there's something hanging out of my locker," said Elizabeth, walking ahead of Justin.

A piece of folded yellow paper was wedged in the crack of the door. Elizabeth unfolded it and read the note. "It's working. Our plan is working!" she said. She grabbed Justin's sleeve and pulled him closer to see the note, which read:

You have something that belongs to me.
I want it back.

"Doesn't tell us much," said Justin. "It's paper from a legal pad, and it's written in pencil."

"It tells us that whoever stole the ring goes to school here and saw it today. The thief must have accidentally dropped it and wants it back. I wonder why the thief didn't say anything about *how* to give it back."

Justin shrugged. "Maybe the person's feeling guilty and doesn't want you to know who he or she is. Anyway, all we've managed to do so far is narrow down the number of people who could have taken the ring to everyone in this school," he said. "What about questioning everyone whose dad is a lawyer and uses a legal pad?"

"We can check the handwriting," Elizabeth said. "Do some snooping and see if you can find a match." She took the *Dear* ring off and tucked it in the pocket of her backpack. It felt good to take it off. She'd been feeling guilty all day about wearing a ring that wasn't really hers.

"Yes, ma'am, but first I have to deliver some newspapers," said Justin.

"And I need to stop by Read It Again and see if Teresa needs me," said Elizabeth.

"Where's Meghan?" Justin asked.

"She must be sick or something. I haven't seen her since lunch."

"That's why it's been so quiet," said Justin

with a grin. He waved and took off down the hall.

Elizabeth continued to stare at the note after Justin left, hoping that it would tell her something.

"Love note?" Christy asked.

Startled, Elizabeth crumpled the paper.

"Want to hang around downtown with us?" Heather asked.

"We're looking for something to wear to the party Friday," said Sarah.

"What kind of party is it?" asked Elizabeth.

"Usual. Nothing special," said Heather. "But I'm tired of all the old things in my closet. It's a good excuse to get something new."

Sarah and Christy nodded their heads in agreement.

"It won't matter much what you're wearing once the lights go off," said Christy. The three girls giggled.

It suddenly struck Elizabeth how much alike the three of them looked. All had shoulder-length straight hair, different colors but the same style—parted on the side with wispy bangs brushed back. Each wore jeans and a plaid shirt, again different colors. Elizabeth suddenly felt like her red hair was too bright and too curly and her T-shirt too childish.

"I have to work," Elizabeth said, wishing she didn't. "But we could walk together."

"Work!" exclaimed Christy.

"At Read It Again. The bookstore."

"Must be boring," said Sarah.

"But easy," added Heather.

Elizabeth shrugged. She looked around for Meghan, then remembered that she'd been absent.

"Elizabeth, where's your ring?" Christy asked.

"In my bag," Elizabeth said, wishing she hadn't taken it off so quickly.

"Your mom doesn't know?" asked Heather.

"Nope, not yet," Elizabeth said.

"Mothers!" said Sarah, shaking her head. "Too uncool."

Elizabeth smiled and said nothing.

As they walked downtown, the girls talked about clothes with an occasional comment about boys. Elizabeth said little, not having much to add.

"This is it," Elizabeth said when they reached the bookstore.

"Let's go in," said Christy. "Your turn, Sarah."

"For what?" Elizabeth asked. The three girls exchanged looks.

"If Elizabeth starts hanging with us, that'll make four," said Sarah.

"Four what?" Elizabeth asked.

"We'll let you know when the time is right," said Christy.

Elizabeth jerked the door open. It was clear she wasn't part of the group yet. "Teresa, it's me," Elizabeth called out as they entered the store.

"Hi, luv. No deliveries again, I'm afraid." Teresa walked toward the girls, her orange curls dancing. "You've brought me additional bibliophiles."

Christy and Heather giggled. Sarah wandered away. Elizabeth felt her face burn. She'd always thought Teresa odd, but she liked her anyway. It felt funny to have other people looking at her like she was weird. "This is Christy and Heather. That's Sarah," Elizabeth said, pointing to each girl. "This is Teresa Smythe. She owns the store."

"Nice to meetcha," Christy said.

Suddenly, Heather jumped into the air, giving short shrieks as she hopped around. "Mouse! A mouse! Crawling up my leg," Heather cried.

Christy doubled over laughing. "It's a cat," she said. "A fuzzy cat."

"Almost as bad," Heather said, rubbing her jeans where Finola had shed. Finola huddled under a nearby table. "Cats are so hairy. Ick."

Teresa was staring at Heather open-mouthed. Elizabeth was beginning to feel like it wasn't a very good idea to bring her friends in to meet Teresa. They didn't have much in common.

Sarah rejoined the group. "Let's go," she said.

"You ready?" Christy asked her. Sarah nodded.

"Sorry you're stuck here," Christy whispered as they filed out. "Maybe tomorrow."

"Are you going to church tonight?" Elizabeth asked Christy.

Christy glanced at Sarah and Heather, then shrugged.

"Well, if you do, I'll see you there later," Elizabeth said, realizing she'd picked exactly the wrong thing to ask. She felt a sense of relief when the door shut behind the group.

"Interesting friends. Quite unlike Meghan and Amy Catherine," Teresa said.

"They are, but I've known Christy forever," said Elizabeth, searching for a way to change the subject. "Is there anything I can do?"

"Business is a little slow," said Teresa.

"I may look for something to read," said Elizabeth. Teresa was nice about letting her borrow books. There was a mystery by Carol Gorman she wanted to read. Elizabeth went to the shelf to find it.

"Teresa, have you seen *Die for Me?*" Elizabeth asked.

"I don't think so," said Teresa. She joined Elizabeth. "Perhaps someone sampled it and laid it elsewhere."

"That's okay. I'll pick it up later," said Elizabeth. Between homework and youth group, she wouldn't have much chance to read tonight anyway.

"Odd. I haven't noticed any young people in here today other than you and your friends," said Teresa. "When I come across it, I'll set it aside for you."

"Thanks. Guess I'll go."

"Thank you, luv, for checking in," Teresa called as Elizabeth walked out the door. Teresa waved as she walked by the window.

When she passed the jewelry store, it reminded Elizabeth of her mother and Mr. Hamilton. A diamond ring usually meant an engagement and then marriage. Mr. Hamilton would move in with them, wouldn't he? They couldn't move away from Aunt Nan. She'd lived in the duplex next to them for as long as Elizabeth could remember. Aunt Nan was a member of the family. Mom's closet was full and so was her dresser. Where would Mr. Hamilton put his clothes? She didn't want to think about it.

"I'm home," Elizabeth called out.

"Hi, sweetie. How was your day?" Mom yelled from the kitchen.

"Okay," Elizabeth said. "Did Meghan call?"

"She did. She left school early. Poor thing, she has the flu," said Mom.

Elizabeth's cat, Tiger, greeted her with a meow. She stooped to pet him. "How could anyone think you're icky?" she asked the cat.

"Don't make any plans for Friday night," Mom said.

Friday. That was the night of Heather's

party. "I already have plans," said Elizabeth. The idea of the party had been dangling there, just out of reach, but so tempting.

"You'll have to cancel. This is important—a put-on-your-best-party-dress and high-heeled shoes kind of night," said Mom.

"You won't let me wear high heels," said Elizabeth.

Mom laughed. "We're going to Schneithorsts for dinner. Strudel for dessert."

Schneithorsts. Elizabeth had only been there once before, when her grandmother came to visit. "What's the occasion? Is Grandma coming?"

"No. A special night for you, me, Mike, and Don. And maybe Aunt Nan," said Mom.

Don. A special night. It set off alarm bells in Elizabeth's brain.

7

Thou Shalt Not

"Why do you always let me out so far away?" asked Elizabeth as Mom stopped the car in the middle of the church's empty parking lot.

"Is this close enough?" Mom asked, pulling up to the door of the parish hall.

Elizabeth climbed out of the car. "Eight o'clock," she said. Meghan's mom usually picked them up after youth group so she wanted to be sure Mom knew the right time.

A car pulled close to Mom's and honked. Mom and Mrs. Singer exchanged waves as Christy joined Elizabeth at the door.

"You came," said Elizabeth.

"Keeps Mom happy," replied Christy with a shrug.

Inside the hall, Elizabeth waved at several people she saw only at church and started toward a group gathered around the snack table. Christy grabbed her arm and dragged her to a far corner of the room. "Come over here. I want to show you something."

"I wanted to tell ..."

"Look at this." Christy pulled a necklace out of her shirt. P-U-G, spelled out in rhinestones, twinkled in the bright lights. "Cool, huh?"

"What does *PUG* stand for anyway?" Elizabeth asked.

"Heather and Sarah have one too. We had them made at Ring Doodle," said Christy, avoiding Elizabeth's question. "My mom said it was better than a tattoo."

"But ..."

"Kids, take a seat someplace," Ms. Halliday called out. "I have someone I'd like you to meet and make welcome."

Christy sat down at the closest end of the half-circle, away from most of the group. Elizabeth hated sitting apart from the rest of the kids, but she didn't want to leave Christy sitting completely alone. She took a seat next to her.

"This is Judy Clark, your new leader," Ms. Halliday said.

Elizabeth started clapping before she

looked up to see Ms. Clark. Her hands fell to her lap. Ms. Clark was the salesclerk from Ring Doodle who had accused her of shoplifting!

"She works at Ring Doodle," whispered Christy. "Maybe we'll get discounts."

The woman was dressed in jeans and a sweater and looked younger than she had in the store. As her smile swept the circle, Elizabeth slid down in her chair, hoping Ms. Clark wouldn't recognize her.

Ms. Clark turned to look at Elizabeth a second time. For a moment she looked confused, then the smile faded. Elizabeth knew she'd made the connection between her and the shoplifting incidents.

"Tonight we continue our study of the Ten Commandments with 'You shall not steal,'" Ms. Halliday said.

Elizabeth couldn't imagine the situation getting any worse. Again, she felt Ms. Clark's eyes on her. She tried to sit still despite the urge to squirm.

The door opened, taking everyone's attention away from Ms. Halliday. Matt stepped inside.

"I can't believe he came," Christy whispered to Elizabeth. "I dared him. Why doesn't the J-Man come with you?"

Elizabeth had invited Justin to come with her many times, but he always had an excuse. Still, she wouldn't give up. He'd come a long way from the Justin who changed the subject every time she mentioned God, Jesus, or prayer. Sometimes he even brought up the topic.

Matt stood in the doorway, looking around the room. He jerked his hat off as he looked at one after another bareheaded boy. Maybe that was why Justin wouldn't come, Elizabeth thought. She'd hardly ever seen him without a baseball cap.

Finally, Matt's eyes landed on Christy. With a nod to Ms. Halliday, he headed straight toward them, plopping down in the empty chair on the other side of Christy. She shifted slightly closer to him and whispered in his ear. Matt slumped in his chair, staring at the floor.

"Before we get too far into our activity tonight, we need to take care of some business. I need updated phone numbers and addresses," said Ms. Halliday. She rummaged through a stack of papers on the table. "I seem to have forgotten the sheet, however, ..."

Christy pulled her backpack around and reached inside. She held up a yellow legal pad and a pencil. Elizabeth had to swallow quickly to stifle her gasp.

Matt scribbled his name and address, then Christy. Grabbing the pad almost before Christy finished, Elizabeth studied the handwriting. Matt's didn't match. It was too small, almost unreadable. The writing on the note had been what? Elizabeth tried to come up with a word and decided on precise. Christy had written her name and address in cursive, clearly and neatly. Neither seemed right. At least the paper definitely matched.

"Can I have some volunteers?" Elizabeth heard Ms. Halliday say when she tuned back in. For what, she wondered. Christy bumped Elizabeth's elbow, causing her arm to raise slightly.

"Elizabeth, great. Come on up here," Ms. Halliday said.

Matt and Christy bent double in silent laughter as Elizabeth reluctantly joined the group in the center of the half-circle. She wished she knew what they were going to do.

Ms. Halliday took the legal pad Elizabeth was still holding and passed it to the next person in the circle.

"This is your situation," Ms. Clark said, taking over. "You are in a store and see two people you know from school. As you are talking to them, you see one slip a package of gum in her pocket. What do you do?" Ms. Clark stepped back.

"Who's supposed to be the different parts?" asked Ryan, one of the other volunteers.

"I guess that might help," said Ms. Clark with a laugh. "You be the person who sees the shoplifting. You be one of the friends," the leader said, pointing to Geri. "And you be the shoplifter." Ms. Clark was pointing at Elizabeth.

Elizabeth felt a surge of anger toward Christy. She wouldn't have been up here with Ms. Clark practically telling the group that she thought Elizabeth was a shoplifter if it wasn't for Christy.

"Hi, Ryan," said Geri.

"Hi. What are you two doing?"

"Just hanging out. What about you?"

Elizabeth listened to the two of them, adding nothing to the conversation. Finally, Ryan looked at Elizabeth and said, "I think you might have knocked some gum into your pocket accidentally."

"You know, you're right," Elizabeth said, feigning surprise. "I'll pay for it before I forget."

"Ryan, why did you put it that way?" Ms. Clark asked.

"I couldn't imagine *Elizabeth* stealing anything," he said.

The kids laughed, and Elizabeth wanted to hug him, she was so grateful for what he said. Ms. Clark, on the other hand, didn't look pleased.

"It's just a roleplaying exercise," she said.

"Let me try," said Christy, jumping up. "But let's make the stakes a little higher. This time Elizabeth is going to ..."

"No, Elizabeth has had her turn. Let's get some more volunteers," said Ms. Halliday. She called Amanda to the center of the group. Elizabeth took an empty seat next to Ryan, leaving Matt alone on the other side of the half-circle.

"This time you see a friend take a necklace, and then she tries to give it to you as a gift," said Ms. Clark. "You be the thief, Amanda. You be the friend, Christy."

After pretending to open the gift, Christy said, "I can't take this. I saw you shoplift it from

Ring Doodle. It says in the Bible that it's wrong to steal. I'll go with you to take it back."

The group clapped, and Christy curtseyed.

"Could you say that in real life?" Ms. Clark asked.

"I would have said something the minute I saw her take the necklace," Christy said very seriously.

Ms. Clark smiled and patted Christy on the shoulder. "I'm sure you would."

Elizabeth squirmed in her seat. This role-play situation was a little too similar to how she got her friendship ring. Maybe she should take it back tomorrow and admit to Ms. Clark how she got it and why she didn't bring it back right away.

As soon as Christy sat down, she and Matt whispered back and forth, then laughed. Elizabeth wondered if Christy even noticed that she'd changed seats.

Throughout the evening, Ms. Clark continued to look at Elizabeth each time she mentioned shoplifting, which she did a lot. By the end of the meeting, Elizabeth had a stomachache.

Hearing how the other kids reacted to the

roleplaying, Elizabeth couldn't imagine that anyone—including Matt—would even consider shoplifting. She decided the right thing to do was to return the ring—as soon as she could explain her decision to Justin.

8

The Ring Tightens

Elizabeth checked her locker at lunchtime, hoping for another note from the ring thief. She still hadn't had a chance to talk to Justin about returning the ring, but she also hadn't given up the hope that the person who stole it would somehow make himself or herself known. It would save her from having to face Ms. Clark. Elizabeth still wasn't sure the woman would believe that she hadn't taken the ring.

With Meghan still sick, Elizabeth dreaded going to the cafeteria. Sitting all alone was no fun. Elizabeth stood at the entrance to the lunchroom, sweeping the large, noisy crowd, hoping to quickly sight her friend Amy Catherine to sit with her.

"Liz! Hey, over here," she heard a girl yell.

Amy Catherine was so tall she usually was

easy to find in a crowd of seventh-graders, but Elizabeth couldn't see any trace of her. She toyed with the idea of spending the lunch hour in the bathroom or coming up with an excuse to visit her mother, a language arts teacher at the school.

A hand clasped her arm. "What's wrong with you? Can't you hear?" Christy asked. "We've been yelling our brains out trying to get your attention. C'mon over here."

Christy led Elizabeth to a long table. "Scoot down," she said to a small girl with very short dark hair. "This is Liz. She's going out with Justin. Show them your ring."

Elizabeth sat down at the end of the table. Several girls she recognized from classes but didn't know very well looked at her— the ring really—for a moment then returned to their conversation. Elizabeth took out her sandwich and unwrapped it. The other girls seemed more interested in talking than eating.

"We didn't find what we were looking for yesterday so we're going to the mall tonight. Want to come?" Christy asked.

Of course, Elizabeth had just taken a big bite out of her sandwich. She shook her head and held up her finger as she quickly chewed.

"Can't," she said. "I have dance class tonight."

"You *still* take dance?" Christy wore a look of amazement. "You and Sarah."

"I like it."

"Me too," said Sarah.

"Have you decided what to wear Friday night? You *are* coming, aren't you?" Christy asked.

Elizabeth remembered her mom's command performance but couldn't bring herself to say no to Heather's party yet. The lunch table she'd joined was a beehive of activity in the middle of the cafeteria. Other kids looked at them often yet stayed away. She was one of them—the party-up girls, the PUGs—minus the necklace. She realized Sarah, Heather, and Christy wore theirs proudly.

Maybe she could do both—dinner with Mom then the party. "I may be a little late," Elizabeth said.

"Better not leave Justin alone *too* long. He's hot," said Christy.

Elizabeth managed to smile thinking about what Justin would say about being tagged "hot." Still, she didn't like hearing Christy say it.

"Anybody want to read this?" Sarah tossed

a book in the middle of the table. The crowd groaned almost in unison.

"Who has time to read?" Heather asked.

Elizabeth twisted to see what book it was. *Die for Me!* The same book she'd tried to find at Read It Again. "Have you read it?" Elizabeth asked Sarah.

"I skimmed it. It looked pretty good."

"Where'd you get it?"

"Ummm. Can't remember exactly where I picked it up," said Sarah.

Elizabeth noticed that a few giggles met that comment. "Can I borrow it?" she asked, pulling the book toward her.

"Keep it," Sarah answered.

Again giggles, then an exchange of glances between the kids at the table. Elizabeth felt squirmy and out of it, like they knew something she didn't know—something about *her.*

The lunch bell rang. The girls around the table groaned.

"If you have a chance, catch up with us at the mall later," Christy said.

Elizabeth gathered her trash, noticing most of the people she'd sat with left theirs on the table. One more trip to the locker, Elizabeth decided, as she walked out of the cafeteria. She hurried and was rewarded with a folded sheet of paper stuck in the hinge.

> *Thou shalt not steal* ***MY*** *ring. I'll catch up with you.*

The message gave Elizabeth a chill. At youth group, they had discussed the commandment and now this note. She quickly ran through who had been at the meeting, hesitating at Matt. He'd only come to see Christy, yet he'd been very convincing during his turn at role-playing. He also had been at Ring Doodle.

Sticking the note in her backpack, Elizabeth decided she had enough time to stop by the bathroom and still make it to class on time. She hustled down the hallway.

"You don't want to go to class either?" Heather asked as Elizabeth entered the girl's bathroom. Sarah was with Heather. The two of them were perched on the window sill. Heather played with her necklace. Sarah was doodling on a—yellow legal pad!

Elizabeth quickly positioned herself to be able to see Sarah's handwriting. It was large and loopy, definitely no match for the writing on the notes. Elizabeth had never realized how many people used legal pads instead of notebook paper.

"I just need to wash my hands," Elizabeth explained. She slipped off the ring and laid it on the shelf above the sink, worried that the soap would dull the shiny stones. After washing her hands, Elizabeth glanced at her watch and decided to use the facilities.

"Justin's coming to my party, isn't he?" Heather asked her through the door.

"As far as I know," said Elizabeth. She heard the girls whisper and again felt uncomfortable. The swinging door swished opened then shut, and silence filled the room.

Washing her hands again, Elizabeth remembered the ring. Her eyes darted to the spot on the shelf where she'd laid it. Empty!

"Okay, where's the ring?" she asked the empty room as she dried her hands and tried to keep the beginnings of panic at bay.

If Heather or Sarah had taken it, Elizabeth didn't think the joke was very funny. She continued to look for it, dropping to her knees and searching the not-too-clean floor.

The drains. What if it had fallen down the

drain? Elizabeth stuck her fingers into the sink opening as far as they'd fit. "Ugh! I hope not." She rinsed her hand.

On the edge of the farthest sink, Elizabeth spotted the ring and quickly slipped it back on her finger. Why had she ever taken it off? The ring wasn't even hers, and she'd almost lost it.

The bell rang again. Elizabeth grabbed her backpack and rushed to class, still wondering how her ring had moved from one sink to the other.

Elizabeth took the long way to her locker after school, hoping to run into Justin along the way. She wanted him to go with her to return the ring. As Elizabeth walked past the office, she noticed a man lounging against the counter, talking to the secretary. He was swinging a pair of sunglasses by the earpiece.

Elizabeth stopped and backed up a few steps, taking a second look at the man. He put the sunglasses on and she recognized him—the shoplifter.

She slipped around the corner and waited, taking a peek every few minutes to see what the man was up to. She wasn't sure what she was going to do next, but she didn't want to let him get away again.

Elizabeth was so intent on watching the man that when a hand touched her neck, she jumped away, turning and striking out.

"Hey! What'd I do?" Justin asked, backing away and holding his hands in front of his face.

"It's only you!" Elizabeth said, leaning against the wall for support. "He's here."

"He? He who?" Justin looked all around.

"The man with the sunglasses. From Ring Doodle. The shoplifter."

"Here?"

"In the office," said Elizabeth. She looked around the corner again. Mrs. Magnusson was busy typing. "He *was* there, talking to the secretary."

"How do you know it was him?" Justin asked, looking for himself.

"How did I know? I'll *never* forget him," said Elizabeth. "It's like he's burned into my brain. I'm surprised I haven't had nightmares about him."

"Let's ask Mrs. Mag who he is." Justin covered the short distance to the office and pushed open the door.

Mrs. Magnusson looked up from her keyboard. "Hi, Justin, school's out. What are you doing hanging out here?"

"That guy you were talking to a minute ago. Who was he?" asked Justin.

Elizabeth crowded in the doorway beside Justin. "The one with the sunglasses," she added.

"I don't remember anyone wearing sunglasses," said Mrs. Magnusson, not looking at them.

Justin and Elizabeth exchanged glances. That was the shortest answer Mrs. Mag had ever given to any question.

"He just left. He was leaning against the counter," Elizabeth pressed her for an answer.

"He must have been somebody for Mr. Brown," Mrs. Mag said, staring at the computer screen.

"Has he ever been here before?" Justin asked.

"I don't know. So many people come through here," answered the secretary.

And you remember every one of them, thought Elizabeth. Mrs. Magnusson could recite the names of students from the first year the school opened. The keys on the computer keyboard clicked as Mrs. Magnusson turned away.

"Thanks," said Elizabeth. As the glass door shut, she and Justin looked at one another.

"That's weird. Mrs. Mag usually can't tell you enough," said Elizabeth. "And I got another note."

"Coincidence," said Justin.

"Maybe," said Elizabeth, "but I'm ready to take the ring back."

"Why?"

"Ms. Clark, that's the woman who works at Ring Doodle, is our new youth leader at church. Guess what the topic was last night."

"Shoplifting?" guessed Justin.

"Every kind of stealing you could think of—borrowing without permission, sampling, finding stuff, plagiarism." Elizabeth ticked them off on her fingers. "I'm worried I'm breathing someone else's air."

"So you're feeling guilty about the ring?" asked Justin.

"I have been all along, but I almost couldn't sleep last night. What if I lose it and can't return it? or scratch it? or lose one of the stones?"

"Okay, take it back. It won't hurt my feelings. Besides ..." Justin looked away. "I mean, the ring doesn't mean anything."

Elizabeth felt like she'd been punched.

"No, I don't mean that either," said Justin quickly. "I'm not good at this stuff. I don't like you anymore with a ring than without, okay?"

Justin looked like one of her cats when it knew it had done something wrong, but not what it had done. Elizabeth would have laughed, but that would make Justin feel worse, and right then she didn't know if she could feel any better.

"Will you ... I was kind of thinking ... could you go with me? To return the ring, I mean," Elizabeth said.

"Today? Now? I'm already late for basketball practice," said Justin. "Could Meghan go?"

"Still sick. I guess I could wait till tomorrow. You know, I have to walk home by myself, eat lunch alone ..."

"You ate with Christy and that bunch today," said Justin.

"It was nice of them to ask me, I guess. Can you go to Heather's party Friday?" Elizabeth asked. Remembering the invitation lifted her spirits. She decided returning the ring had to wait, *should* wait. The note meant someone was looking for it. And what if Heather wouldn't want her to come to the party without a ring?

"You *want* to go?" Justin looked surprised.

"Kind of," Elizabeth admitted. "Don't you ever wonder what they *do?*" She could already hear the buzz in the halls on Monday with her name and Justin's among the ones everyone was talking about. Besides, that was one of the things about going out with someone, getting invited to the parties.

"Nope," said Justin.

"Then you don't want to go?" Elizabeth felt a flood of disappointment. Justin had just said he liked her.

"I'll go if you want to," said Justin.

"Great, but I'm going to be late. I have to go out to dinner with Mom and Mr. Hamilton." A picture of Mom trying on engagement rings flashed on, then off in front of Elizabeth's eyes.

"Mr. Hamilton? What happened to Don?" Justin asked.

Elizabeth shrugged. Justin was another Don Hamilton fan and wouldn't understand. It seemed to Elizabeth that she barely got used to one change before she was pushed into another.

She'd finally decided Don was okay to have around and now Mom was thinking of *marrying* him. Or was she? Mom still hadn't said anything about an engagement ring.

"What's wrong?" Justin asked.

Elizabeth cleared her head of thoughts about Mom and smiled at Justin. "Nothing. Don't you have practice?"

"Sure do. See you later. You working?"

"Not tonight. I have tap class," said Elizabeth. With a wave, Justin headed out the door.

By the time Elizabeth had all her books packed in her backpack, the hallway was quiet and empty. The silence was strange. Each step Elizabeth took echoed, giving her the creeps. She glanced over her shoulder. All the classroom doors were closed, and most of the lights had been turned off. Elizabeth walked a little faster, causing the sound of her steps to echo even louder. She stopped, but the footsteps continued.

9 Thief in the Night

Elizabeth twisted the ring on her finger, thinking about the man with the sunglasses right here at school. She pressed against the wall waiting for some clue as to where the footsteps were coming from.

"My ring," a whispery voice called to Elizabeth. It seemed to come from the far end of the hall.

Keeping close to the wall, Elizabeth sidled away from the voice. She took a deep breath, realizing she'd barely breathed while she waited for the voice to speak again.

"Elizabeth." This voice was full force and familiar.

"Hi, Mom." Relief swept over her.

"You're kind of late tonight. Need a ride home?" Mom asked.

"Justin and I were talking." Elizabeth realized she still had the ring on and hoped Mom wouldn't notice before she had a chance to take it off.

The sound of running footsteps reached them, coming from the far end of the hall. Elizabeth turned, hoping to catch a glimpse of the body that went with the voice, but no one appeared. A door slammed shut.

"Another late one," said Mom. Elizabeth wasn't so sure.

"How about that ride?" Mom asked again.

"Okay." Elizabeth followed Mom to the car, unable to stop looking over her shoulder.

"Don is picking up Mike at school and taking him to buy new shoes," Mom said.

"Nice," said Elizabeth. She only half-listened to Mom going on and on about her classes. Who had been in that hallway with her? And how far was he—or she—willing to go to get the ring? Elizabeth glanced at her hand.

"Hey, where'd that come from?" Mom grabbed Elizabeth's hand and looked at the ring.

Chewing her lip, Elizabeth tried to decide what to tell Mom. It would be such a relief to unload the whole story and ask Mom to help her take care of things. But wouldn't talking about the ring be a perfect chance for Mom to tell Elizabeth about *her* ring?

"What is wrong with you, Lizzybeth?" Mom asked. "You seem to be a million miles away."

"Justin gave it to me," Elizabeth said.

"What does it mean?"

"Mean? What does it mean?" Elizabeth repeated.

"Are you going steady? Boyfriend, girlfriend? What?" Mom asked.

"We're *not* engaged," Elizabeth said, hinting.

Mom laughed. "That's a relief."

"It means we're going out," said Elizabeth.

"Out where?"

"Mom, you know what it means. We're invited to a party Friday night," Elizabeth said.

"But you said no. We're all going out to dinner," Mom reminded her.

"I said I might be late to the party," answered Elizabeth.

"I think you'd better tell your hostess that you won't be there at all. I'm not sure I approve of boy-girl parties for a child your age ..."

"Mom!"

"You and Justin have gotten along so well as *friends.* I hate to see you change direction and maybe lose that. Besides this dinner is a special dinner," Mom explained.

"What's so special about going out to eat?" Elizabeth turned away and stared out the car window. "So I can't go even *after* dinner? This is the first time I've been invited."

"We'll see," Mom said as they turned into the driveway. Elizabeth pushed the car door open as soon as the car stopped.

"Oh, I forgot to pick up milk," said Mom. "I think I'll go now. Want to come along?"

"Is Aunt Nan home?" Elizabeth asked. Maybe she could ask Aunt Nan to put in a good word with Mom.

"I don't know."

Elizabeth got out of the car. "I think I'll visit with her a while. Plus I have some homework to do before dance class tonight."

"Be back soon," said Mom.

Elizabeth knocked on Aunt Nan's door. No one answered. She tried the knob, but it was locked. She opened their side of the duplex and went inside. The blank TV screen looked inviting. It would be nice to watch something and forget all about the ring, Mom and Don, the dinner, the party.

The phone rang. Elizabeth grabbed it, hoping it was Meghan.

"You still have my ring. I want it back," a voice whispered. Then Elizabeth heard a click and the dial tone.

Boy or girl? Elizabeth couldn't decide. She hung up the receiver and quickly locked the door. Then she threw herself on the sofa and clicked on the TV. She needed a break.

"I may be a little late picking you up," Mom said as Elizabeth got out of the car at the dance studio. "I have an errand, and I don't know how long it will take. I thought you could get a ride home with Meghan."

"She's still sick," Elizabeth said.

"I'll try to be on time, but just wait if I'm not here," said Mom.

Elizabeth slammed the car door. Inside the dance studio, she changed her shoes, took the floor, and started stretching. Sarah, who had never even spoken to her in class before, moved from the back of the class to the front row beside

Elizabeth.

"Is that a ring I see?" Miss Karen asked.

Slipping the ring off her finger, Elizabeth ran to the side of the room and stuck it inside her bag. She was getting too used to wearing it. Without the ring, her hand felt light, like it was going to float away.

Sarah rolled her eyes when Elizabeth took her place in line.

Dance class worked much better than TV had at getting Elizabeth's mind off her problems. She decided to take the ring back to the store on Monday, after she and Justin had gone to one good party, even if she hadn't figured out who had stolen it and convinced the culprit to return it. The party would be a perfect place to talk to her prime suspect, Matt. Since he was going out with Christy, he'd certainly be there.

"She's something," said Sarah, pointing at Miss Karen with her head.

"A really good teacher," said Elizabeth.

"I guess," said Sarah, "but the *rules.*"

"Uh-huh," said Elizabeth. She didn't think that Miss Karen's rules were so bad. Dance meant discipline.

"My mom will be mad if she has to wait for

me," said Sarah, jumping up off the floor, jeans on over her leotard and shoes tied before Elizabeth even had her tap shoes off. "See you tomorrow."

"Hey! You took my bag," Elizabeth yelled after her.

"Sorry." Sarah tossed it toward Elizabeth and disappeared out the door.

Elizabeth dressed slowly, not wanting to have to wait for Mom any longer than she had to. She looked outside—no sign of the car. The cool air felt so good, she decided to wait on the sidewalk. One by one the girls in her class were picked up. Elizabeth stepped back inside the studio.

"You still here?" asked Miss Karen. She had on jeans, and her purse was slung over her shoulder.

"My mom's late. I can wait outside," said Elizabeth.

"I hate to leave you here alone," said Miss Karen.

Elizabeth could hear an anxious tone in her voice. "It's okay," she assured her teacher. "She'll be here any minute."

"Josh is with a sitter who told me she had to leave on time tonight," Miss Karen said apologetically.

"Go, go," said Elizabeth, backing out the door.

"I don't like ... I could drop you off," offered Miss Karen as she locked up the studio.

"Mom is on her way. Go on home," Elizabeth said again. "See you next week."

Miss Karen waved as she pulled away from the curb.

Elizabeth paced back and forth in front of the dance studio, irritated with her mother. An occasional car passed, but Elizabeth was the only person on the street. She threw her dance bag to the ground and kicked it in frustration. It felt good.

The next thing Elizabeth knew she was face down on the concrete sidewalk, her palms and knees stinging from where they'd hit the rough surface. When she looked behind her to try to figure out what had happened, a figure holding her dance bag melted into the darkness between the buildings.

Just then, Don Hamilton's car pulled up to the curb.

"Honey, we're sorry to be so late. Why are you sitting there on the sidewalk?" Mom asked.

"Someone just pushed me down and stole my dance bag," Elizabeth said, "with my shoes in it." She stood up and set off toward the alley. A hand grabbed her and held her.

"Let go!" Elizabeth cried, trying to pull away from Don. "I want that bag."

"You don't know who's down there," Don said.

"It was just a kid, a girl," Elizabeth said, surprising herself with her knowledge. But the figure appeared in her mind—slight, with a glint of light bouncing off long, shiny hair.

"I don't care who it was. You're not going down that alley in the dark," said Don firmly.

Mom joined them and shined a flashlight into the dark.

"There! My bag," said Elizabeth, pointing. She freed herself and lunged for it. "Empty! It's empty."

Mom and Don joined her, Mom playing the light along the pathway. "Here's a tap shoe and your ballet slippers," she said.

"Another tap shoe," said Don.

"Did you have anything else in the bag?" Mom picked up a pink leg warmer and dusted it off.

With a sinking feeling, Elizabeth realized there was something else. She turned the bag inside out and then dropped to her knees, feeling along the ground with her bare hands. "The ring," Elizabeth said, "the *Dear* ring."

10

MALL LESSONS

"Your ring. *Where* is your ring?" Christy cried out as she met Elizabeth at her locker before first hour.

Elizabeth groaned. She, Mom, and Don had crawled over every inch of the alley without success. Even though she knew it was illogical, Elizabeth felt like she *had* stolen the ring now that she'd lost it and couldn't return it as she'd planned.

"You didn't break up already?" Christy asked in a voice that caused heads all up and down the hall to turn.

"No," said Elizabeth. "My dance bag was stolen after class last night, and the ring was in it."

"Too bad," said Christy.

"We got the bag back and my dance shoes but not the ring," said Elizabeth. She would go back, after school, and look again.

"Bummer," Christy said. "J-Man will have to get you another one."

"I don't think so," said Elizabeth. She shut her locker door and started walking toward her first class.

"Of course he will," said Christy, falling into step with Elizabeth.

Elizabeth let it go. Justin couldn't afford to buy her the first one, but Christy didn't know that.

"Listen. Heather, Sarah, and I want to invite you to a little preparty this afternoon, after school," Christy said.

"After school?"

"Just for a while. At the mall. You *have* to come."

"Let me check. Remember I'm going to be late for the party," said Elizabeth.

"I know. You've told us a million times," said Christy. "What about J-Man? Will he be late too?"

"Justin?" Elizabeth said. "I'm not sure." The J-Man thing was getting on her nerves.

"My mom is driving us to the mall so meet us at the front door as soon after school as you can. We need to pick up a few things for tonight. Plus we have something real important to show you," said Christy as Elizabeth turned into her classroom.

Elizabeth skipped lunch to talk Mom into letting her go to the mall. Having a mother who was a teacher at the same school worked out some days—especially when Mom said yes.

Christy, Heather, and Sarah were already in the Singer's station wagon when Elizabeth came out of the school building.

"C'mon slowpoke," Christy yelled out the front window. Heather scooted into the middle of the backseat to make room for Elizabeth.

"Finally," said Mrs. Singer, pulling away from the curb. A car honked and brakes screeched. Elizabeth snapped her seat belt.

"I have an appointment at 3:30. I told you that, Christy," said Mrs. Singer.

"Will you be able to pick us up?" Christy asked.

"You told me you had a ride home," Mrs. Singer said.

"My mom's working," said Heather.

"My mom doesn't drive," said Sarah.

"Maybe my mom can come," said Elizabeth, thinking of the dinner reservation. "But we can't stay long. I know Mom has plans."

"You mean a date," said Heather, smirking.

"With Mr. Hamilton?" asked Sarah.

Elizabeth felt herself blush. Mom's dates weren't exactly her favorite topic of conversation. "We're all going out to dinner," she said.

"How could we have forgotten?" asked Christy.

"Your mother is dating?" asked Mrs. Singer. "How long has your dad been gone?"

Gone? Like he was on a trip, thought Elizabeth. "My dad died about five years ago," she said.

"Here. Let us out here," Christy demanded. Mrs. Singer stopped the car in the traffic lane, causing more horn honking as the girls piled out.

"I need to *pick up* some earrings. What about you, Heather? What are you picking up?" Christy asked, giggling. The three girls staggered together, laughing.

"Maybe I'll *pick up* some lipstick," said Heather.

"I need a new thingy to pull my hair back

with," said Sarah.

"Okay, Elizabeth, what about you?" asked Christy.

"I don't need anything," said Elizabeth, having that "missing something" feeling again.

"Yeah, right," said Christy, and the threesome laughed again.

"First stop, Carmels," Sarah said. The three girls linked arms and moved forward, not bothering to make way for other people in the mall. When Elizabeth hung back, Christy grabbed her and linked her arm through Elizabeth's.

"Guys, we're pushing people out of the way," said Elizabeth, mouthing sorry to the mother pushing a stroller who had to dodge out of their way.

"So?" said Heather. "They can see us and move."

Elizabeth began to wish she hadn't come.

At Carmels, an earring boutique, the girls spread out. Elizabeth looked at a pair of small gold earrings shaped like ballet slippers and at some others that looked like sunflowers.

"C'mere." Christy motioned for Elizabeth to join her. "Like these?" Christy held a cat earring to her ear. It reached halfway to her shoulder.

"Kinda big," mumbled Elizabeth.

"I like dangly earrings," said Christy. She turned away.

Elizabeth wandered to the wall where hair accessories were displayed. Sarah was riffling through a rack of large bows.

"I like that one," said Elizabeth, pointing to a red one.

"This would look better in your hair," said Sarah, holding out a navy blue ribbon with silver stars on it.

Elizabeth looked at barrettes until Sarah stumbled into her. "Sorry," said Sarah, giggling again.

"I'm ready," Christy called from the doorway. Everyone joined her.

"You didn't get those earrings?" Elizabeth asked, seeing Christy's empty hands. She wished she'd said the cat earrings were okay.

"Let's just go," said Christy, looking pointedly at the salesclerk standing close by.

"Lipstick time," sang Heather.

"Elizabeth, you don't wear much lipstick," said Sarah.

"I don't wear lipstick at all," said Elizabeth.

"We'll take care of *that,*" said Christy. "I

mean, if you're going to be k-i-s-s-i-n-g the J-Man, you want your lips to be soft and creamy."

The blush that consumed Elizabeth was worse than usual. "I ... I ... ," she stammered.

"C'mon, tonight's the night, girl," Christy said.

Then it was true what everyone said about the parties Heather threw? Elizabeth wondered. It was partly curiosity about the truth of what she'd heard that made her want to go to the party—dark rooms, slow dancing, kissing.

At the cosmetics counter, Heather immediately started testing various colors on her hand. Sarah sniffed colognes, and Christy tried on eye shadow. Elizabeth looked at lipsticks with Heather. Maybe she would buy a tube.

"This one, Fiery Rose, would look good on you," said Heather.

"I'd never get out of the house with that on," said Elizabeth. The lip color was bright and dark. She touched a gold tube of lip gloss. "Maybe this."

"That's for babies," said Heather, dismissing Elizabeth's choice with a wave of the hand.

"Hey, Liz, come take a whiff of this." Sarah squirted cologne into the air and breathed deeply. "It's spicy, yet light. Innocent and sexy at the same time." The girls laughed, and Elizabeth joined in. It was kind of fun to relax and joke.

As soon as she moved within range, Sarah sprayed her with the scent. "Sarah!" Elizabeth backtracked, turning her head to find a breath of plain old air. Out of the corner of her eye, she glimpsed a flash of gold arcing from the lipstick display to Heather's pocket. She whirled around to get a better look, but Heather was handing a gold tube to the salesclerk. How could I even think such a thing? Elizabeth wondered as she watched Heather pay for the lipstick.

"Pizza or ice cream?" asked Christy.

Elizabeth lifted her shirt and smelled the cologne. She was going to have to take a shower to be able to sit at the table with other people. The scent was so strong she could even taste it.

"Pretzel," said Sarah.

"Nothing for me," said Heather. "I must have put on 10 pounds in the last month."

"Everybody get what they want, and we'll meet back at this table," said Christy.

Elizabeth sat down without any food. If they were going out to a big meal, she wanted to be hungry.

Heather returned first with a soda. "Diet," she said. "Want a sip?"

Elizabeth wrinkled her nose.

When Sarah and Christy arrived with ice cream *and* pretzels, Heather announced, "Show and tell."

Christy removed the hoop earrings she wore, reached in her pocket, and held up the cats she'd shown Elizabeth earlier. Once in her ears, she turned her head from side to side, showing them off.

She must have bought them when I was looking at hair clips, Elizabeth thought.

"Cute," said Sarah as she pulled her hair back and secured it with a big black bow.

Elizabeth cleared her throat uncomfortably. When had Sarah bought that bow? She realized her foot was tapping madly. She crossed her legs at the ankle, uncrossed them, and planted her feet firmly on the floor, pressing on her knees with her hands.

"Here, Liz, for you." Heather tossed a gold tube at her.

Elizabeth put her hand up to keep it from hitting her in the face. "I can't take this," she said. "I know it cost a bunch."

Heather shook her head. "I *picked it up* for you."

"Nail polish to match," said Sarah, setting a bottle down in front of Elizabeth.

"Where'd you get it?" Elizabeth had to force the words out. The three girls laughed.

Elizabeth pushed the lipstick and nail polish away and leaned back. "You stole these things," she whispered.

"Just picked them up," said Sarah, smiling broadly.

"It's a little game we play," Christy said. "We're the Pick-Up Girls." She traced the letters on her necklace. Then she dangled a matching necklace in front of Elizabeth. "And here's one for you. All you have to do is pass the initiation test."

"Which is?" Elizabeth asked, knowing and dreading the answer.

"Be a pick-up girl," said Christy. "Anything you want."

"It's stealing," Elizabeth said, looking around, hoping no one was listening to the conversation.

"They're just little things. We're not hurting anybody. Stores build this stuff into their prices anyway," said Heather. "They *expect* it."

"I can't believe you did this," said Elizabeth. "I'm taking it back." She reached for the lipstick and nail polish, but Sarah was faster.

"What is wrong with you?" Heather asked. "We want you to be part of our group."

"It's ... it's ... wrong," Elizabeth burst out, amazed that she had to explain herself, justify herself.

"Look, we come to the mall and each of us picks up one *little* thing," said Christy. "I guess you could call it a club. And we want you to be a member." Christy's eyes were round and serious as she leaned close to Elizabeth.

"No." Elizabeth shook her head. "Christy, how can you not know how wrong this is? You've gone to the same Sunday school as me forever."

"Her mom *makes* her go," said Heather.

Christy's head dropped.

"Take the earrings back," Elizabeth urged her. "Pay for them. How can you wear them knowing you *stole* them?"

"How did you wear this?" Sarah tossed the missing ring onto the table. It clattered loudly.

"You!" Elizabeth exclaimed. Sarah must

have waited after she left dance to grab her bag. It must not have been an accident that she picked it up in the first place.

"That ring wasn't Justin's to give to you in the first place," said Christy.

"I was the one accused of stealing that ring," Elizabeth said. "And the notes, the phone calls, those were mean." Elizabeth leaned back in her chair and crossed her arms in front of her chest.

"Now we're mean. Boo-hoo," said Heather. "And what are you going to do about it?"

Elizabeth pushed back her chair, taking Heather's words as a challenge. "I'm turning you in," she said.

"How will you explain what's in your pocket?" Sarah asked.

Elizabeth patted her pocket, then stuck her hand inside and pulled out the star-studded navy bow.

"I told you guys she was a goody-goody," said Sarah. "Aren't you glad I thought ahead and protected us?"

"So what now?" asked Heather, smiling.

Elizabeth realized that Heather's smile wasn't pretty as she'd once thought, but nasty.

Elizabeth looked directly at Christy, who refused to look at her. The earrings, she noticed, were laying on the table alongside the ring, lipstick, and the nail polish. Lord, please help me stand up for what's right, Elizabeth prayed silently.

"I'm going to do something I should have done a long time ago—leave. I don't want to be part of your club. It's wrong, and you all know it," Elizabeth said as she turned away. "I hope you guys change your minds and pay for those things before someone gets into real trouble."

Elizabeth was trembling with anger as she walked away. "Thank You, Lord, for letting me find out what was going on," she said under her breath. "Please show me how to help Christy and be her friend."

As she left the group, Elizabeth heard Heather say, "Okay, Christy, now you'll have another chance at Justin. No way she'll come to the party tonight."

Heather was right about that, Elizabeth thought. She felt a tiny twinge at the thought of Christy and Justin together.

Elizabeth dug some change out of her purse and called Mom to come pick her up. Thankfully, Mom promised to come right away.

When Elizabeth passed the table where they'd all sat, the girls and the goods were gone. All that was left was one PUG necklace.

Elizabeth stuffed her hands in her pockets. The bow was still there. As hard as it would be, she knew she had to take it back. It would be good practice for telling Ms. Clark what had happened to the ring.

At Carmels, Elizabeth stopped at the door. Christy was at the cash register counting change into the outstretched hand of the salesclerk.

"Here," Elizabeth said, joining them. "I need to pay for this."

"I guess you 'accidentally' carried that off too," said the clerk.

"She didn't know it was in her pocket," Christy said quickly.

"Hmph," the clerk sniffed. "$4.24."

Elizabeth gave her a five.

"I'll pay you back," Christy said.

When she had her change, Elizabeth turned to leave. She couldn't wait to get away from the looks the salesclerk was giving them.

"I'm sorry," said Christy. "You were right. I did feel bad when I took things, but Sarah and Heather made so much fun of me ..."

"People made fun of Jesus too," said Elizabeth. She sighed. "He didn't give in to temptation though."

"Are you going to tell your mother?" Christy asked. She looked almost ready to cry. "She'll tell mine and I'll be in so much trouble."

"Do you have the ring?" Elizabeth asked. Christy nodded and held it out to Elizabeth.

"Take it back and tell Ms. Clark you took it."

"I can't!" Christy protested.

"But she thinks *I* took it."

Christy opened and closed her fingers around the ring. "I'll try," she said.

Elizabeth sighed. "I'll go with you. Any chance you can go now?" She didn't want to put it off any longer.

"You will?" Christy's eyes grew wide, and her lips stopped trembling. "I guess I can. I don't exactly have anything to do."

"There's Mom. We'll ask her to take us," said Elizabeth.

"Hi, Christy," Mom said warmly. "Long time no see."

"Hi, Mrs. Bryan," Christy answered from the backseat. She leaned down, arranging and rearranging her backpack, refusing to look at

Mom.

"I know that time is a problem, but could you drop us off at Ring Doodle for just a minute?" Elizabeth asked.

"Our dinner reservations ..."

"I know. I wouldn't ask if it wasn't really, really important." If Mom knew why, she'd take them, Elizabeth thought, but she'd rather talk about it with Mom when Christy wasn't around.

Mom sighed. "If you take longer than 10 minutes, I'll come in and drag you out—in front of all your friends."

"Thanks, Mom." Elizabeth leaned over and kissed her on the cheek.

The trip to Ring Doodle was silent.

Mom double-parked then said, "Ten minutes. I mean it. I'm going to drive around the block to see if I can find a parking space."

Elizabeth and Christy climbed out of the car, Christy clutching her backpack and Elizabeth empty-handed.

When she took a good look at Christy, Elizabeth got a little scared. The girl's face was so pale it was almost green.

"Are you all right?" Elizabeth asked her, touching Christy's hand and not feeling very reassured by its cold dampness. Christy squeezed Elizabeth's fingers.

"I always get an upset stomach when I'm nervous," Christy explained.

Elizabeth pulled her fingers free and bent them to make sure Christy hadn't damaged them. "You aren't going to throw up, are you?"

Christy shook her head. "I don't think so," she whispered, then amended, "at least not now."

Great, thought Elizabeth, as if this whole thing wasn't already bad enough.

The irritating music played when the door opened. Ms. Clark looked away from the man she was helping, her back stiffening when she saw Elizabeth.

The man turned, and Elizabeth's mouth dropped open. She recognized him even without his sunglasses—the shoplifter.

11 Confession

"It's him! He's the one who took the earrings, Ms. Clark," Elizabeth said without hesitation. She shook her finger at him as she backed out the door, intending to yell for help.

In two steps, the man had hold of her arm. Christy swung her backpack, but he deflected it with his free hand.

"Girls, wait a minute," Ms. Clark said. "He didn't take the earrings."

"He did! I saw him!" Elizabeth twisted and turned, trying to get free. She lifted her foot to kick him in the shins.

"He's *Officer* Morison," Ms. Clark said, rushing from behind the counter and grabbing Christy before she could swing the bag again.

Elizabeth would have fallen if the man wasn't holding her, she stopped her kick so fast. She stumbled when he let go of her arm.

"A police officer!" Elizabeth said, still not believing.

"The owner of the store hired him to test how well we were watching for shoplifters. And I didn't do a very good job," said Ms. Clark. "That's one of the reasons I was so upset with you."

"Why didn't Mrs. Mag tell us who you were?" Elizabeth asked.

Officer Morison shrugged. "I was asking her about you so maybe she thought it was a secret. She assured me you wouldn't shoplift."

Elizabeth's face burned. Mrs. Mag, and who else, knew about the ring?

"Believe me, I'm convinced you didn't take it," said Ms. Clark. "Everyone was outraged I'd even think such a thing about you."

Elizabeth looked at Christy. Christy looked at Officer Morison, then back at Elizabeth. Elizabeth recognized the fear in her eyes. "You promised," Elizabeth said.

Christy slowly opened her backpack and reached inside. "Elizabeth didn't take the ring. I did." She set it on the counter.

"But I had the ring for a couple days. Instead of bringing it back, I tried to use it to make the real thief come forward. I know I should have brought it back right away," Elizabeth admitted.

Officer Morison cleared his throat.

"I know this won't mean much, but I'm sorry and I won't do it ever again," said Christy. Her voice was barely audible.

The police officer looked at Ms. Clark. "I can't let her go without any punishment," said the salesclerk.

"Maybe we can work something out," said Officer Morison.

"I'll pay for the ring. But I don't want it," said Christy. She pushed it away from her. "Does my mom have to know?"

The officer nodded. Christy bit her lip, and tears welled in her eyes.

"I'll talk to my mom, and maybe she'll talk to yours," said Elizabeth.

Christy nodded and as her head tipped, the tears rolled down her cheeks.

A horn honked. Elizabeth knew it had to be her mom.

"You go on," Christy said, her voice husky.

"I don't want to leave you all alone," said Elizabeth.

"It's amazing," said Christy. "You have every right to hate me, and yet you're here while the people I thought were my friends are," she snapped her fingers, "gone."

"I'm glad to be your friend," Elizabeth said with a smile. "We'll get this mess straightened out."

"Bringing the ring back helped," said Officer Morison.

"If the police weren't already here, I would have handled this my way," said Ms. Clark.

"How?" Officer Morison asked.

"Community service—sorting clothes for the church rummage sale. I'm in charge," said Ms. Clark.

Christy wrinkled her nose but said, "When do I need to show up?"

"How about 9 A.M.? But you still have to tell your mom," said Ms. Clark. Christy nodded.

"And next time, I won't be wearing shades." Officer Morison took the sunglasses out of his pocket and put them on.

"There won't be a next time," Christy and Elizabeth said together. Christy smiled weakly.

The car horn sounded again.

"I'll help you tell your mom, after church on

Sunday. We'll talk about it tomorrow when we sort the donations," said Ms. Clark.

"Elizabeth, go on. I'll walk home from here," said Christy.

"You sure?"

Christy nodded.

Ms. Clark followed Elizabeth to the door. "I owe you an apology," she said. "I am sorry, and I hope we can start over."

Elizabeth smiled. "Apology accepted," she said. Forgiveness granted, she thought. How good it feels to be able to forgive. Thanks, Jesus.

12 Going Out

Even though it was a good feeling to solve a mystery, there was always a sad part to it, Elizabeth thought. People who were supposed to be her friends had set her up, threatened her, and most of all, disappointed her.

"Okay, what was that all about?" Mom asked as Elizabeth got into the car.

"It's kind of a long story," Elizabeth said.

"You aren't wearing your ring," said Mom.

Elizabeth shook her head. "It was never mine. Christy stole it and lost it. The lady at the store accused me of stealing it, then Justin found it and gave it to me. I knew it was stolen and decided to find the person who did it. I'm kind of sorry to know."

"Christy? Christy Singer stole something?"

"Stole lots of stuff, Mom. She and her friends had a club called the Pick-Up Girls. It meant that they picked up stuff without paying for it."

"Carol isn't going to be very happy about this," said Mom.

"I told Christy maybe you'd talk to her mom. I don't think Christy will steal again," said Elizabeth.

"I'll think and pray about it," said Mom. "We don't have long to get ready for our big date. Why didn't you tell me about this earlier?"

"You were so busy ..."

Mom sighed long and loud. "I'm never too busy for you."

"I know, but I told you now," said Elizabeth.

"Somehow I'm not sure I know everything," said Mom as she pulled into the driveway.

"I'll tell you the rest when we have a little more time. Dibs on the shower," Elizabeth said, hopping out of the car and running up the porch steps.

"Already had mine," Mom sang out.

"You ladies look lovely tonight," Don said when Elizabeth came down the steps.

Elizabeth had to admit that her mom looked

pretty good. Her hair was loose, just touching her shoulders, and the red dress she had on was just right.

"What about me?" Mike asked.

"Handsome is what I'd call you," said Don.

Mike threw his shoulders back and stood next to Don, his hands in his pockets just like the older man's.

"We're going to be late," said Mom.

"First, I want everyone to sit down a minute," said Don.

Elizabeth's stomach started to feel funny. "I'm really hungry," she said, knowing that wasn't why her stomach felt the way it did.

"This will only take a minute, I hope," said Don. He pulled a long burgundy velvet box out of his jacket pocket. "Elizabeth, Mike, Lydia, I'd like to ask you to marry me."

He opened the box. Inside there was a gold Mickey Mouse watch, a gold cross necklace, and a diamond engagement ring.

Elizabeth looked at Mom. Mom's face was flushed, but she wore a smile that made any other light in the room unnecessary.

"Which one is mine?" Mike asked, pulling the box down and looking at the jewelry. Don

Hamilton took the watch out and fastened it on Mike's wrist.

"Cool," said Mike. "Are you going to get us a wedding present too?"

"I guess that's one yes," said Don, laughing. He turned to Elizabeth.

Mom had hold of Don's arm. "Honey?" she asked in a hopeful voice.

Elizabeth felt tears burning behind her eyes, but she smiled as best she could and nodded.

Don fastened the cross around her neck. Elizabeth fingered the delicate necklace as thoughts rushed through her mind. A cross. Did that mean Don was beginning to think more about Jesus? Surely Mom wouldn't marry someone who wasn't a Christian.

And what about everything that had just happened? She'd come awfully close to putting up with shoplifting. Thankfully, Jesus had given His life for her mistakes. Help me not to make a mistake about Don and Mom, she asked Him silently.

Elizabeth came back to the present with a start as Don looked into Mom's eyes. Taking the ring out of the box, he got down on one knee and slipped it on Mom's finger.

"Why are they doing that?" Mike asked. "Are we getting married tonight?"

"Not that soon," said Mom.

"When?" Elizabeth asked, hoping her voice didn't give away how little she wanted this to happen. Mom and Mike—and Don—looked so happy.

"We can decide that later," said Mom.

"Not too much later," said Don, putting his arm around Mom and pulling her tightly against his side. He planted a kiss on top of her head. "Now we *really* have something to celebrate."

"You can sleep in my bedroom in the top bunk when you marry us," said Mike. "No, I'll sleep on top. You might make it fall down and then I'd be smushed."

Mom and Don laughed again. Elizabeth's stomach growled loudly. She put her hand over it, like that would quiet it.

"Time to eat," said Mom.

Don held the door open and they filed out in front of him, Elizabeth last. As she went by him, he grabbed her arm. "Thanks," he said. "I was a little worried about what you'd say."

"I probably couldn't live here anymore if I'd said no," said Elizabeth, immediately wishing she hadn't.

"I know I can't take the place of your father, and I'm not even going to try. But I promise to be the best guy who's married to your mom and living in your house that I can be. Okay?"

Elizabeth's stomach growled again.

"And as God is my witness, you'll never be hungry again," Don said.

Elizabeth couldn't help but laugh. "That's from *Gone with the Wind,*" she said. "How do you know that?"

"I'm not completely ignorant. I go to the movies," he said, shutting the door behind them.